Romeo 1

LOVE...?

To learn about
Love!

Romeo
19.05.21

2020

First published in the United Kingdom in 2020 by Romeo Leu.

ISBN 978-1-8380754-3-9

British Library Cataloguing-in Publication Data. A catalogue record for this book is available from the British Library

Translation from Romanian language by: © Luiza Cornelia Varovici

Cover design and cover graphics: © Luiza Cornelia Varovici

Computer editing: Romeo-Marin Leu

Photo of the author by Clifton Photographic Company

Printed in the United Kingdom by:

Inky Little Fingers Ltd

Written and typed (in Romanian language) by the author in 2017 in:

Chania and Malia, Crete, Greece; in Buziaș, Timișoara and Lugoj, Jud. Timiș, and in Gura Portiței, Jud. Tulcea, Romania

LOVE...?

Romeo Leu
2020

I dedicate this book to all the women who helped me understand better what love is. I believe that it is only in the power of women to cast more light on this subject, untaught, controversial, and perhaps difficult to understand.

Success to all the seekers in love...

Chapter 1

The night was slowly falling over the small village in the South-West. The sun had descended behind the hills for over an hour ago, and in the sky, the stars began to flicker fiercely. The silence contained the whole village. From time to time, a solitary bark gave the impression of a deserted place. People worked hard in the field all day, so they went to bed early in the evening, with the hens, as they say. Even the lights on the house windows were off and, along the way, only a dim light bulb shed some light in front of the Police Station. Even the tavern in the village was closed, and at the Grocery store only a small bedside lamp lit the display window full of household items, canned food, sugar bags and flour.

Walking on the lane in the middle of the village, guided only by the light of the stars, you could see a strange light beyond its northern end. It was about five hundred meters away from the limit of the village towards the Red Hill. At the end of an old dirt road, a wooden house with a stone foundation emerges. It had a shingle roof, and the small windows were divided into square glass panels. The large door, semi-rounded at the top, was made of solid wood that seemed to be stolen from an old castle, making a special, even discordant note with the rest of the house. There was no fence around it, and behind the house there was only an old brick hearth on which stood a huge three-legged trivet.

The yellow iridescent green light spilling through all the glass squares, made it impossible for any attempt to look inside. The surroundings and even the house were engulfed by this phosphorescent light.

Nobody in the village bothered about this strange light. First of all, it only appeared after the majority of the villagers were asleep. Secondly, the house was not in the village, so both administratively and even technically, the village had nothing to do with this house. Finally, the villagers did not believe those who said they saw this light, for the only ones who saw it were the well-known alcoholics of the village. These, given the high degree of drunkenness, instead of going from the tavern towards their homes, took the opposite direction, out of the village and consequently getting closer to this mysterious house.

Even though the house next to the Red Hill was outside of the village, people knew the two women living it. Mother and daughter, they had lived there for quite a long time, but time seemed of no value to them.

The old lady was always present at the fair in the village selling the mushrooms that she had picked, according to her, from the woods. She was also selling all sorts of herbs and roots for medicinal teas and other medicinal remedies. All „gathered from the woods", although the forest was a few hours away on the opposite side of the Red Hill.

This woman had a strange appearance with her white curly hair standing on her head like a badly wrapped broom; she always wore a black kerchief around her neck and a black dress with long sleeves, ripped and patched, long to the ground but also wide. It was virtually impossible to see any shape of her body under these clothes. Her small hands, with long and dry fingers, seemed to be huge claws attached to thin and skeletal arms. Her black eyes like charcoal big and sunken, made her face impossible to look at for more than a moment, and her large mouth with a lot of missing teeth, along with a sharp chin, completed the horrifying picture of this lady.

Nobody could remember where this old lady and her daughter had come from, or when they had settled in the house at the foot of the Red Hill. At the same time, no one could claim that she had harmed anyone or did anything dangerous for the village. Everybody bought mushrooms and remedies from her and were very pleased, though no one wondered how a woman of a seemingly venerable age could go such a long distance to gather mushrooms and plants in order to sell them three times a week on the days of the fair, Tuesday, Thursday and Saturday.

As for her daughter, they knew even less of her although she was much more present in the village world, because she was involved in many so-called cultural activities. Day in and day out, this young woman showed herself to be very faithful and eager to help the village churches the best that she could, but especially through her participation in the choir in all the sermons.

Having neither husband nor children, she was the youngest of the choir, but also the most eager to repeat and sing without a mistake. Due to this she was noticed, for otherwise she was a tall and dry woman with a long but pleasant face. Her brown eyes with light green flecks, gave her an almost poetic look. Large lips, luscious and lightly opened were inviting you to kiss her constantly. The tiny, barely shaped breasts gave her a virginal appearance amplified by the narrow hips and the flat and saggy bum. The thin legs could hardly be seen, because most of the time they were covered either by a skirt or a dress long to the ground, or with some wide and straight trousers. Her talk was melodious, even sweet one could say, and when she was singing, her voice was warm but resonant.

Therefore, both the village women and the men noticed the tall thin girl with a resonant voice in between the prayers of the local Pastor. I said Pastor because I forgot to say: there were two churches, a Traditional Christian and a Neo-Protestant one, in the small village in the South-West. At present, our daughter sang in the choir of the Neo-Protestant church, but in the past, she also sang for the young priest of the Traditional Christian Church.

As for the names of these women, no one bothered to discover their origin or family, and because they did not have a man to take care of them, they were called by the so-called baptismal name. The oldest was Baba Rada and the younger Florentina. No one could be sure these were their real names, but as long as everyone called them so, these were their names.

And so these women led their lives at the margin of the village in the South-West being so „visible" that no one could actually say what they were doing, but that still remains to be told, of course, if you will have the patience to read what follows next.

Chapter 2

At the end of a late summer, Anuța (spelled Anutsa /aɳʊʈa/) was tending to her father's sheep on a beautiful meadow in the mountains. It was sometime in the afternoon and leaning on her father's heavy staff, she was waiting for her father to come back. He had left before the lunch hour to go to the nearest hamlet to bring bread and some vegetables for the two weeks that they still had to stay on the „Heaven's doorsill", high in the mountains. She wasn't afraid of or had any trouble to being a shepherdess. Although she was only 16, her father had taken her to the sheepfold for more than ten years. He had taught her all that she knew: to write, to read and to count, but especially the craft of the sheep, how to care for them, sheer them, milk them, and how to make the wonderful cheese so sought after by the people on the plains. Her father, the shepherd, felt that she would be the heir of the flock of ewe-lambs since her birth, when he was informed by his wife's midwife that he had a girl as his heir. Of course, he wanted her married to another shepherd, with a bigger flock of sheep and thus to make together a magnificent huge flock like no one else.

Anuța was not thinking of this as she knew that her father had already found her husband to be, but as every girl she **was dreaming of a lover** in the like of a fairy-tale Prince. While the sheep quietly grazed and the dogs ran around without barking, holding them in a circle, Anuța was dreaming of her Prince seeing herself dancing with him to the sound of wonderful music dressed in a white bridal dress, as she had seen in a magazine from the city. But if one of the dogs barked while she daydreamed, she would have to cry out for a stray sheep or to lift the staff threateningly at the sight of a wild beast. Her father always told her how well off she would be when married to the rich shepherd and how much money they would both have.

This shepherd was a man in his prime that was getting close to 40 springs. He was a bachelor, in the mountains since he had been young, like her, next to his father who had died a few years earlier confronting a bear one night. Year by year he enlarged his flock and now he wanted to marry a shepherdess in order to get a bigger flock. The name of this shepherd was Ion.

Anuța met Ion only once a few years ago when she was just an innocent child. She remembered only his black moustache and his heavy palms when he stroked her head and kissed her forehead.

Her mother always said that a woman **does not have to love** her husband at first, for **love** comes with time. That is why Anuța was not bothered at all with this proposed union, because she was **in love** with the Prince from her dream.

Before sunset, her father arrived with the donkeys loaded with supplies for the sheepfold. As soon as he got there, she quickly prepared a meal and then they began to share their thoughts as they always did in the evening in the light of the fire in the hearth of the sheepfold.

-Father, she said, *we only have two more weeks to stay in the mountains and then we will descend home...*

She had to stop suddenly as the dogs began to bark forcefully. The shepherd went outside to see what was happening. He returned almost immediately, saying:

-It was nothing, maybe a wolf got close and the dogs scared him away... Yes, my daughter, we will descend and then we will prepare for the wedding.

Anuța went silent in the still of the night and a heavy waiting seemed to fall between them...

*-My daughter, you remember we talked about this, **are you in love with someone else?** Have you committed any dishonour without my knowledge?*

-No father, she answered with a quiet voice. *I'm just not ready to be a wife...*

-Well, you're not ready..., he rebuked.

Anuța put down her head and said in a low tone:

-I will obey you, father, and I will marry Ion.

-That's right, my girl, he said. *You will see that all will be well.*

The night settled in without notice and a night owl was singing ominously from the top of a rock spire... HOOTHOOT... HOOT... HOOT...

The following days passed quickly and in two weeks the ewe-lamb flock together with the shepherd father and his daughter the shepherdess were heading for the village at the foot of the mountains.

Meanwhile Ion, who had arrived earlier in the village, was busy making the wedding preparations. The wine and „țuica" (plum brandy, spelled tsuica) were ready in big barrels and the young lads who were announcing the event were each going with a full flask at the gates of the village people inviting them to the wedding.

Anuța arrived within a few days. Her mother was waiting with the other women in the village to prepare her for the wedding. The priest of the village gathered the children and asked them to help with decorating the interior of the church with flowers. There was agitation everywhere. The future couple did not even get to see each other, and as Anuța asked her mother if she could speak a bit with Ion, her mother replied that she would have a lifetime to talk to him. But for now there are more important issues to resolve, such as the bridal dress, the crown of flowers, the white nightgown and, last but not least, the papers for her dowry - all the flock of sheep with dogs and donkeys and all as it had been agreed between the groom and father-in-law. Anuţa being a bit disappointed with this entire flurry was not in the mood nor had any time to dream of her fairy-tale Prince. She felt trapped in a vortex that seemed to drag her down, down, further down. She said to her mother:

-I'd like to talk to Father Gherasim before the wedding.

Her mother stopped her sewing and looked at her, terrified...

-Did anything happen, my daughter?

-Nothing happened, mother, I would just like to confess before the wedding.

-Do you have any sins, my daughter?

-Mother, please, let me speak to the Priest.

-All right go now. He should be in the church.

Anuţa went hurriedly. She felt that the world was spinning around her like at the fair when she first went on the big wheel. She did not know Ion at all, **did not love** him and did not know a great deal about him. It did not make any sense to marry him. It seemed that the whole village was against her, starting with her parents and family, up to the last stranger who wanted to drink at her wedding in honour of the newlyweds. No, Father Gherasim could not be against her. He baptized her when she was a wisp of a child and he knew her since she was unborn in her mother's womb. Her last hope was in him only. She entered hesitantly in the cool church and falling to her knees in front of the Holy Virgin icon, she began to pray zealously:

-Most gracious Virgin Mary, Mother of God, have mercy on me the sinner; Holy Virgin please guide me, show me the path and send me a sign if it is meant for me to marry this man – Ion.

Her prayer was interrupted by Father Gherasim.

-What are you doing here my daughter?

-Father...

-Did you come to pray at the Holy Virgin for a happy marriage and a fertile womb?

-No Father...

-What words are these?

-Father, in fact I came to confer with you and to confess.

-What are your sins, my daughter? And how can I advise you?

-Father, I only have one sin. You know Father, there at the sheepfold, night after night alone, I mated in my dream and in my thoughts with a fairy-tale Prince. I have sinned in my mind and in fact with this ghost a dozen times. I cannot get it out of my mind; and when my hands run over my virgin body, I feel his passionate kisses burning everywhere. I cannot marry Ion. I feel it would be dishonest for me to think of my Prince when he would want to mate with me... This is my sin, Father. Help me please. Tell me what to do? I feel that a big whirlpool has caught me and that I cannot pull back. The whole village is against me...

-My daughter, don't strain yourself, said the Father. *Many sin so in their maidenhood. It was just a delusion and God will forgive you – I absolve you from this sin. Now get ready to become a woman and you will see that after you feel the palms of a real man on your body, you will forget your phantasy. Come on, go in a hurry, and get ready and you will see that after the wedding night you will see that I am right.*

Anuţa did not dare to ask another thing and thanked the Father by crossing herself. Then crossing herself anew, she backed out of the church.

Going home with her head down, she did not notice how all of the sudden a woman she did not know

16

appeared as if from nowhere. She looked straight in her eyes and in a low voice she said:

*With whom you **do not love**,*

Don't keep your company!

*With whom you **would love**,*

Do keep your company!

Suddenly the woman turned her back on her and vanished as quickly as she had appeared. Anuța burst into tears and started to run towards the house. On the doorstep her mother was waiting and seeing her tired and weeping talked to her nicely and Anuța told her everything. Her mother picked basil from the garden, put garlic on the windowsill and spitting three times performed a spell; then she said:

*-Come on, leave it, it will be all right, **you will love** Ion and you will forget all the evil that happened to you now.*

Hearing all this Anuța calmed down, although the thought that the vision of the woman on the road could be the sign that she asked from the Holy Virgin continued to trouble her. She lay on the bed and went to sleep and hurried back to her Prince. She had not dreamt of him for a long time. Everything was spinning and her body was struggling in spasms. For the first time, among the caresses and kisses, the prince spoke:

*- **My beloved** Queen, I am your predestined, and although I have no flesh, I **can love you** as no mortal can. I know **you love me** too, and that's why I'll always wait for you...*

Anuța suddenly woke up and arose out of the wet bed sheets. She ran to the corner icon, lit the candle, and prayed for the chasing away of demons and evil spirits. She was afraid to tell the story to anyone, and after a while she went back to sleep.

The days that followed passed quickly and at the end of the week the wedding took place. Anuța felt she was in a dream and it was not she who was getting married. Even when the Father asked her if she wanted to take Ion as her husband, the YES statement came out of her mouth automatically without her seeming to have said it.

The whole village was eating and dancing vigorously. The fiddlers were applying themselves to please all the wedding guests with their favourite songs and the kitchen women were bustling to cook and to bring to the tables more and more delicious dishes. Everybody was laughing and making merry. Ion was proud of his young and beautiful bride. Anuța, adorned in her sparkling white dress, seemed to be a real angel fallen from the sky.

The night fell quickly and, according to the tradition the bride and groom retired to fulfil the mating ritual. In their room, prepared ahead of time and adorned with fragrant flowers, the bridegroom, only in his trousers, was looking at his chosen one as she took off her bridal dress and put on the white night gown, which was as white as the foam of the milk. Then he held her in his arms and his heavy palms began to caress her. Anuța did not feel anything at first but closed her eyes and left herself to his will. Only now she was his wife. While his palms descended on her smooth skin, Anuța felt like a faint and soon lost her senses...

-My daughter, what happened? How do you feel?

-I don't know, mother, I was taken ill and fainted. But why am I naked in the bedding?

-Ion is dancing with your nightgown, my daughter, and all the guests are delighted that you were a virgin. Let mom help you get dressed and put the kerchief on your head, as you are a wife now. The maidenhood is over, my daughter!

After these words, Anuța began to get dressed and returned to the party to the cheers of those present.

Towards morning the wedding party subsided and slowly everybody started for their homes. After the last people left, Anuța and Ion retired to their room. They looked at each other like two strangers who had met for the first time. She looked at his firm face dominated by a black moustache, and his steel-coloured eyes, like two bottomless lakes, bored into her eyes. Looking at her virginal body and smiling, Ion said:

-Listen you woman, I hope I didn't leave you with child, I don't have time for children right now!

Anuța was petrified. She did not even know how to react to his words. Anyhow she could not recollect a thing and was embarrassed to tell him that their entire wedding was like a bad dream for her, a dream that luckily was over now. She decided to turn her back on him without a word and got into the bed.

The morning sun shot bright rays through the window curtains, and Anuța, although very tired, had not slept at all. Ion got dressed and walked out of the room. After a while she got up as well. When she asked about him, she found out that he had gone to her home. She found him sharing a shot of „țuica" with her father. They laughed loudly and judging on how they were speaking, they seemed to be quite „inebriated". Her father was saying:

-Here Ion, now that I gave you all that I have most precious, my flock of ewes, along with the shepherdess as well, I want you to promise me my boy that you will look after them. From now on I will live on what I put aside.

-Well, father-in-law, said Ion, *this was our bargain. Rest assured that I will take care of the flock like the apple of my eye. Nothing is dearer to my heart than the sheep, father-in-law. I will ask my wife to guard them at the cost of her life. Let's drink for that!*

The glasses clinked loudly!

Upon hearing how much her father and husband **loved her**, she decided on the spot; she took only her shepherd staff and ran for the woods behind the house. Pledging her **love** for the Prince, she ran nimbly among the young trees in the morning light. In a few hours, when the sun was already high into the sky, she was far away from the village. Knowing all too well the footpaths of the forest, she proceeded slowly to the mountains in which she grew up. She passed through a small hamlet where people knew her and asking for victuals on credit, everyone gave her more than enough, including a haversack. Towards evening she reached a rocky slope where she knew a cave. This is where she hid from her father when he beat her or scolded her for something that he thought she did wrong when she was just a child.

She entered the cool cave and gathering fir branches she rapidly made a warm bed. Then she ate in silence. Looked upon from the mouth of the cave, the sun was setting majestically over a landscape that took your breath away. For the first time Anuţa felt free.

A free woman!

Chapter 3

Ion returned home „three sheets to the wind" and when he saw the bedroom empty and all the things of his new wife untouched, he thought that Anuța might be outside. Tired from all the effort and drunkenness, he threw himself on the bed and went to sleep instantly.

The following day though, seeing that Anuța was not to be found, he thought that maybe she slept over-night at her parents. He looked for her there, but nobody knew her whereabouts. The news fell like a thunderclap. Everybody in the village spoke only about Anuța's mys-terious disappearance. All sorts of rumours started to circulate that she was kidnapped for ransom, that she **ran away with a lover**, that she killed herself somewhere or even that she went away from home into wandering the wide world. Everybody talked about it, but nobody was doing anything. Father Gherasim, entreated by Anuța's mother, asked the villagers inclined to do a good deed to organize a search in the surrounding areas. As for her new husband Ion, he was desperate that he had lost his shepherdess and now there was no one to lead his ewes. Her father was still incapable of understanding what had happened being still under the influence of alcohol.

The searches done reluctantly were soon finished, much to the despair of Anuța's mother. Everyone reassured her saying that her daughter would surely return, seeing that they had not yet found her dead body some-where. Concerning her father, she was no longer in his care being Ion's wife. As for Ion, he was happy about handsomely enlarging his flock and he was busy now looking into hiring a few shepherds to lead it. The life in the village at the foot of the mountains got back on its track and the mysterious disappearance of Anuța was soon forgotten.

Meanwhile all this time Anuța roamed the moun-tains, knowing the paths, the hamlets, and their people. From time to time she stopped at one or the other of the villagers to help with the fruit gathering or picking grapes at a vineyard. She helped even with the sheep when people needed, as she was very skilled in making cheese. The people paid sometimes with money, or at other times just with food and accommodation. But eve-rywhere she was well received as she was industrious and full of kindness. On the other hand, she started to feel that something changed in her body. When seeing her, an elderly woman asked her:

-Daughter, do you know that you are with child?

Completely befuddled, Anuța confessed that she was married for one day and it could well be that in the short time that she did not get much out of it she got pregnant. The woman laughed and said:

*-Yes, my daughter, but this could also be a „**love story**" ...*

Anuța did not know what to answer but she thought that she **did not love** her husband at all; she had not even got to know him properly. The woman advised her on what she had to do from now on and how to care for her unborn baby. Anuța thanked her and slowly, slowly she got used to the idea that one day she would be a mother but did not give much thought on how or what would happen.

She thus continued in the following months caressing from time to time her ever growing tummy. Sometimes she felt the small being kicking her feet and in the long winter nights she seemed to hear a whispering in her dream: „Mommy, Mommy..." She somehow knew even from the first months that it will be a girl but her feeling of being sure only came with the spring when the first flowers showed, the white snowdrops, the violets, and the crocuses. She thus decided to call her Florentina (In Bloom) when the baby will be born.

All this while, her **lover** the Prince kept appearing in her dreams, caressing, and kissing her ardently. He did not seem upset at all with Anuța being pregnant and that her tummy was growing with the days that went by. He **always reaffirmed his love** and asked her to meet in his fairy-tale realm. Anuța was intoxicated with the idea that she was **loved** by this apparition and she would do anything to meet him for real and not only in her dreams.

On a hot day at the end of June the time came and, helped only by an old woman in a remote mountain hamlet, Anuța gave birth to a girl that she had named Florentina. She was thin and frail, but with uncommon vitality. She was screaming and always playing with her small hands all day and did not sleep like the other babies. She sucked Anuța's milk avidly and grew up by the minute.

Feeling now relieved of the pregnancy, Anuța became again sprightly and agile, like a deer from the middle of the woods. Her body was back to normal; only the heavy breasts filled with the life-giving milk somehow interfered with her perpetual motion. In a mysterious manner she forgot about Ion completely, even though you would have thought that the constant sight of Florentina would have reminded her of him. It was not like that at all. Tied up in a big kerchief between her breasts or on her back, she carried Florentina all day long working fondly for people to secure her livelihood.

The summer passed and winter came by without notice. She needed shelter. Florentina started to crawl and with the chilly weather it was a bit hard. Anuța decided to find a shelter more secure than the mountain caves, woods or people's granaries from the hamlets and started to ask for lodging. With a small baby she could no longer travel like when she was on her own.

One day, at the border of a village, Florentina met what seemed to be an old woman from her garb and gait. When she looked at her closer, she noticed that the face was familiar, and a tremor came upon her. It was the woman that came across her path in the days before the wedding when she came back from the church. Not wanting to believe her eyes she greeted her saying:

-Good evening, auntie!

-God evening, girl; the woman answered.

-I beg your pardon, but I seem to know you from somewhere, said Anuța with a timorous voice...

The woman did not answer but after a few moments of silence beckoned discreetly to follow her. Anuța, spellbound, followed behind. They walked slowly until after the village border at the foot of a hill. There, suddenly at the end of an old dirt road a wooden house stood on a rock foundation. It had a shingle roof, and the small windows were divided into square glass panels. The large door, semi-rounded at the top, was made of solid wood that seemed to be stolen from an old castle, making a special, even discordant note with the rest of the house. There was no fence around it, and behind the house there was only an old brick hearth on which stood a huge three-legged trivet. Although somewhat scared by this gloomy place, Anuṭa followed the old women without making a sound. As if by magic and without being touched, the big massive wood door opened with a sinister screech. The woman pushed it gently and turning her head said:

-Come inside, my daughter!

Then she entered the house and lit a thick green candle. Anuṭa entered with apprehension. In the candlelight, the house interior looked even more sinister. A long table in a U shape covered three of the room's walls. The table was dominated by some sort of ceramic and glass vases, tied between each other that formed a complicated puzzle. In the middle of the room, on a black stone hearth, some big coals were smouldering. Over the fire and almost extinguished in a big black cauldron that was fixed from the ceiling with three thick chains, a viscous liquid of a violet colour was slowly boiling. Anuṭa was stunned. The woman smiled with a toothless mouth and said:

-Come with me to the room next door. That will be for you and your child.

She opened a small wooden door in the only unoccupied wall, and they entered into a dark room in which there was a fairly big bed, a cupboard and a table with a washbowl and a mug. The woman spoke again:

-Look my daughter, you can stay here as long as you want, and I only want in return that you help me

from time to time with the gathering of healing herbs. I will teach you all that I know and if you wish one day you can be what I am, a wise woman.

Anuța knew some things on the wise women, but never met any of them and moreover, her mother taught her to stay away from them, saying that they were some sort of evil witches. But the offer was too good to be refused and so she said:

-Thank you, auntie, I will think about it. Now I need to leave because I need to gather something to eat for my daughter.

The woman smiled and again in an ingratiating voice added:

-My daughter, if you wished to stay with me, I will bring to you what you hold most precious, your Prince, what do you say?

Anuța was stunned. How did the woman know of her Prince and especially of her ardent wish to be with him, as she had never told her dreams to anyone? Without hesitation she said:

-All right auntie, if you promise to host me and to bring me my Prince, I will stay with you and will serve you the best that I can.

This being said, the big door banged with a big thump closing completely. The current created extinguished the green candle and only the light of the hot coals glittered in the darkness...

Chapter 4

Nothing extraordinary ever happened in the little village in the South-West. Day after day people were working in the fields when it was the time to do so and after that, when on the roadside or when in nearby markets, they tried to sell what they had produced with the help of Mother Earth.

Not the same thing could be said of Baba Rada and her daughter Florentina. Florentina was gathering weeds from the forest and also flowers and mushrooms, „healing herbs" as they are called, and her mother was using them for all sorts of cures aimed at both people and animals. Baba Rada was known for her so-called „healing" powers, but she was doing all other sorts of „works" called spells for special situations. **Love**, money, good luck, or health could be gained or lost according to the customer's wishes and money. As for Florentina, besides her duties of collecting the herbal plants, it was completely up to her to do what she thought fit for the rest of the time. Such that in a noticeably short time she ingratiated herself with the young priest that was serving at the only Traditional Christian church from the small village at the foot of the Red Hill. Although he was married, he could not take his eyes from her small breasts barely shaped, and her brown eyes with green flecks fascinated him immediately, and he could not forget her. Although he knew he was in sin, the young priest did everything he could to see Florentina at least once a day, so he proposed to her without hesitation that she would sing in the church choir. She heartedly accepted and shortly came to lead the choir. Although nothing else happened between them, the priest always had dreams about her and often when he embraced his wife, **swearing his love**, her image metamorphosed by magic into Florentina's image. So, he often asked himself, **what is love?** Florentina in her turn **loved** the young priest madly and in her moments of solitude, in her little dark room next to her mother's room, Florentina fantasized about him by caressing her virginal body. She knew that she could not have him as a husband, but if she asked her mother a little favour, he could be **her lover** at least one night, if not all her life. She did not know what strange event would change the trail of these wishes that seemed to be **love**... but let us leave the story go on...

Almost a month from all these events, in an evening the Pastor of the Neo-Protestant church in the village knocked at the door of Baba Rada's house. His face was transfigured, and the words hardly came out of his mouth. Coming home from a meeting with the believers earlier than usual, he found that the door of his house was open, although he was sure he had locked it himself before leaving for church. For a moment he thought that thieves had robbed him and without making any noise he slowly crept into his own house. Guided by the noises upstairs, he sneaked up towards the bedroom area. Through the open door of the master bedroom, he saw his own wife groaning in the arms of a dark and hairy man, strong as a bear. This brought a lump to his throat.

His wife was supposed to be away from home. He had taken her by car to the train station in the morning of that very day, because she had asked him to leave her for a few days to visit her sick and old mother, who was many hours away. He agreed with her by saying that he could also deal with a few administrative issues in the parish that would take him a few days. They parted on the crowded platform swearing each other **eternal love**... In just a few hours he found her in the arms of another man. It was clear, something was wrong... and now he wanted revenge; he wanted the woman only for himself and the hairy man dead. All **out of love**...

These were said in the small house at the foot of the Red Hill with this clearly stated purpose of revenge. Baba Rada approved and even found the resources to solve the problem. Florentina gazed at him with weepy eyes and **although she was in love with her priest**, the cuckold pastor somehow seemed „sweeter". When he was telling the story of the adultery that he had witnessed, Florentina could sense a gentle warmth that invaded her spine, going down from behind her heart towards the place that once was „Darwin's monkey tail" and somehow she unhurriedly decided that **she loved**

him too... Although she was not very sure, and she had mixed emotions, she said in a weak voice:

-Mother, we need to help this poor lad!

Baba Rada nodded affirmatively and began to boil a hell-broth. Dried skin of poisonous toad, dried leaves of wormwood and dried wings of beetle were all put in the mortar and carefully ground. The resulting powder was slowly boiled in a small cauldron together with a few drops of pigeon blood and some juice of cabbage rotten in salt-free water. The reduced result was dripped into a small glass vial. Baba Rada said:

*-Granny's dear, drop three drops into water or tea that your wife drinks and she will be yours forever. As for him, try to injure him with fist or with knife and dribble at least one drop on the cut and he will be dead in a few minutes. You don't have to injure him yourself if your religion does not allow it. You can ask someone to do this, but the final drop you must drop yourself. You will be revenged and at the same time **rejoice in your love**...*

On the spur of the moment he got terrified and said:

-I don't think I can do this...

Baba Rada looked at him with a smile and said:

*-You will do it because **you love her too much**...*

33

Florentina was watching him wrestle with his thoughts and while she was observing his wet eyes and his fever-ish hand movements, she was more and more sure of her feelings... **she actually loved** the young Pastor. After a few moments of silence, he said:

-*Yes, that's true, I **love her** too much and to her I could do as you asked me, but to him I don't think I am capable...*

-*But you said yourself that you want him dead,* said Baba Rada.

-*Yes, I did,* he said, *but I don't think I can do it. If someone could help me, maybe...*

-*Florentina would gladly help you, what do you say?*

Florentina was startled upon hearing these words – how did her mother know what was inside her soul? Without too much thought, she started to talk in a soft but resolute voice:

-*Pastor, mother is right, I will help you. You just have to describe that man to me, and I will lure him by **telling him that I love him**. Then I will injure him at a convenient moment agreed by both of us and you will fulfil your dream of revenge by dribbling the magic elixir prepared by my mother on the wound. And do you know why I will do all this for you? Only because I just real-ised **how much I love you!** And even if you stay with* *your wife forever, you will always have a **loving and passionate mistress** in me. And I also know that people say that **I love** the young priest, but now I am clear, it is you that **I genuinely love**!*

Baba Rada cut short the amorous declarations by saying:

-It will cost you 5 gold coins. No, I'm kidding, 500 Euros. Do you agree?

-Agree, he said invigorated.

-All right, take the vial and go now. I don't want the village people talking about you being here. Florentina will look you up in order to fulfil the promise...

This being said he left hurriedly.

The next day, around noon, Florentina knocked on the rectory's house next to the Traditional Christian church. The priest's wife opened and after greeting her asked what sort of problem brings her to their house? Florentina told her openly:

*-Madam, I came to tell you that I **found my love** elsewhere and that you can be sure that I **no longer love** your husband the priest, and to be sure of this I will leave the church choir starting today. I pray you convey to the priest all this and if he tries to look for me, it will be only his reverence's sin.*

The priest's wife remained speechless and until Florentina turned away from her she did not manage to utter another word, so they parted without any conflict. **The love „relationship"** with the young priest being thus concluded, Florentina could now focus on **her new love**, the unhappy Pastor. She was not going to think too long about how to achieve this because she already had the solution – she would sing in the choir of the Neo-Protestant church where the Pastor served, just as when she sang for the Traditional Christian church.

With lots of zeal but also false piety she put her black kerchief on her head and quickly entered the place of worship from where Christian music could be overheard. The choir was rehearsing with the music ensemble so she could not have gotten there at a better time. She entered, and as she was not afraid, she went directly to the woman conducting the choir. This one seeing her stopped the choir and greeted her. Florentina said:

-Good day! I don't know if you know me or not, but I decided to repent and in order to serve the Creator's Son I would like to sing in this place and in this choir. I sang for Him before in another church and I don't think that He will be upset that I decided to repent.

Then suddenly she cast her eyes to the ground and gathered her palms beneath her breasts as if in prayer. The woman conducting the choir was stunned for a moment and then said:

-Child, what is your name?

-Florentina, she answered without lifting her eyes from the ground.

-Good, Florentina, I will speak to our brother Pastor and if he will accept your conversion to our worship and baptize you, then you will be able to sing with us. Look, it is Monday today, come on Saturday after the service to speak about all this, all right?

-All right, she said without being able to hide a somewhat wicked smile.

Her plan succeeded. The week passed quickly, time in which she „adapted" her wardrobe a bit according to the garb of the women in the new faith: black kerchief on the head and a long black skirt, down to the ground. She told her mother, Baba Rada, in short, what she was about to do and after receiving her blessing she relaxed completely while waiting for Saturday.

At the appointed hour, after the service, she presented herself at the entrance to the place of worship. The choir lady was waiting for her. Together they went round the church and entered a small annex where the Pastor was preparing to leave.

-Brother Pastor, said the woman, *look, this is the girl that I talked to you about. She wants to be our sister,*

*to embrace our faith and to be baptized in her **love** for God's Son.*

The Pastor lifted his eyes and when he saw Florentina he flinched violently. His heart was pounding powerfully, and he nearly had a heart attack. Of course, the woman mentioned her name, but he had not known what the wise woman's daughter's name was. He quickly gathered himself together and said:

-Of course, my daughter, we have to talk, to prepare you, and then we can perform the baptism.

-Thank you, Pastor, said Florentina smiling, *and when can we start?*

-This very evening you can pass by to talk. Let's say seven o'clock, what do you say?

-I will come, by all means, answered Florentina, visibly invigorated.

The evening fell over the South-West village. Florentina was hurrying towards the Pastor's house; her heart was pounding so fast as if to jump out of her bosom. The Pastor was also anxiously waiting for her. When the clock from the Traditional Christian church spire struck seven, she was in front of the door and he opened it.

-Good evening, she said.

-Good evening. I am so glad you came!

-Me too. I am so nervous. I'd kiss you right here, but I am afraid that your wife could see us.

-No, no, he said smilingly. This time she has really gone to her mother. We are alone here.

Without saying another word, Florentina threw herself at his chest and started kissing him passionately on his face, neck and then mouth. He seemed to be a bit stunned by this and on one hand he got flustered, but on the other he was getting more and more excited. He kissed her very tenderly in response, and then he slowly pushed her aside saying:

*-Florentina, please, I know that **you love me**, but let's take it slowly, shall we?*

-Isn't it true that you are turned on by my body? Come on, please admit it...

-Yes... that is true... but please, let's talk because we have to get organized.

*-All right, **honey**. I will do everything you say.*

-Look, you must learn these verses that I outlined, he said, giving her a small Bible with leather covers. *Afterwards we will schedule your baptism for next week. I will explain everything you have to do when we see each other in a few days.*

LOVE...?

-Ok, ok, but now we have to talk about your problem too, don't we?

-Yes, he said in a barely heard voice...

-Yes, but first where are the five hundred Euros that you owe mother?

-Here, he said quietly, pulling out of the back pocket of his black trousers ten fifty Euro bills.

-Excellent! She exclaimed. *Now I'll tell you how we will execute this. You prepare five hundred Euros more for me and if you agree, we will perform this as I offered to when you were at our house. What do you say?*

-All right, Florentina but I will only give you the money after I see the deed done and the bastard lying dead.

*-Yes, **honey**, that is all right. Come on, tell me what his name is, what he looks like and where can I find him? I hope you found this out, yes?*

*-Yes, Florentina. I had the time to get it out of the adulterous wife of mine. He is a wretched douchebag, who made his money from shell game and afterwards he sold a house left as inheritance by an aunt who **really loved him**. His name is Geo and my wretched wife told me that if she had known that he was such a „bad lay" she would not have gotten involved with him.*

40

-*Honey, how come a „bad lay", you said he is a douchebag.*

-*I don't know, she said that Geo „finished" while she was still undressing.*

-*I understood,* she said.

He continued:

-*Let me tell you what he looks like: he is shorter than you, with a crew cut, he has a narrow forehead and grey steel eyes buried deep in his head. On top of narrow lips, barely contoured, sat a black moustache with the tips down, you know, one of those slick ones. He wears discoloured jeans and white tight t-shirts and, on his feet, of course, white sneakers. Like a real douche that he wants to appear, round his neck and on the right hand, he wears a thick chain and a matching bracelet made out of massive gold.*

-*How sweet,* she flirted. Then she put on the naive look again.

The Pastor glanced at her for a moment and then continued:

-*Yes, you women are all alike, „sweet" is exactly what my wife said.*

-*Don't get angry **honey**, I only said that pejoratively. And tell me, where can I find him?*

-*Well, there's the rub. You see Florentina, he lives in the city because he has an apartment in a block of flats. Supposedly he is a ,,manelist" (low quality oriental-like song player) now and he sings in a restaurant at a central hotel, one of those for foreign people. They say he makes big money there from singing and at weddings. You know this is a big city, the biggest in the West. I have no idea how you will be able to find him there.*

-*Well, **honey**...* she said, *the same way your darling wife did. Tell me now, how did she find him?*

-*Well, in no way! He found her. You know, my wife is a good friend with Ella, the village's primary schoolteacher. She met him there at Ella's house, and as soon as Geo saw her, **he proclaimed his love** to my wretched wife!*

-*I understand, **honey**. Leave it. Let me deal with this now.*

-*And how do you plan we do this?*

-*Oh, easy! Get ready because in two weeks from now we will knock him over. As I said, I will lure him, and you will come at a set time at the place I will tell you. There I will hurt him, and you will drip on him the potion prepared by my dear mother. We will not do this here, but in his big town where nobody knows us.*

-I'm terrified by all this, but I really want it to be finished once and for all.

*-Don't worry, **honey,** because everything will be all right. I **love you** and I will always be with you, **sweet-ie.***

Saying this Florentina clung to his chest and hugged him, kissing him ardently on the mouth.

*-Let me run now, it's late. Good night, **honey!***

-Good night, Florentina!

During the following days Florentina befriended Ella easily because both were now singing in the Neo-Protestant church's choir. In less than a week she managed to meet with Geo and then to start to fill the place left empty by the Pastor's wife. Then the baptism followed and the official entry into the congregation of brothers and sisters of the same confession. She was really happy that she could fulfil her dream of being the Pastor's **lover** and thus she would have an influence over those in her community, only through the **power of love**, as she called it.

On the other side, Geo was more and more attracted by her body and her „**loving**" character. He decided to take her to his place in his big city, where he was going to take her out to restaurants and walks in the famous parks of the city. Everything had been set for the next Thursday, when Florentina was going to take the train to the big city.

Everything seemed to go according to plan and Florentina met in the evening for the last time with **her lover,** the Pastor, before the sought-after event. They discussed everything to the smallest detail, where they were going to meet, how Geo was going to be hurt and then killed and what would happen to the body.

The night was falling quickly, enchantingly lit by the bloody Full Moon that was forecasting everything but well, but **everything being made for and out of love,** did it really matter how everything wood turn out?

Chapter 5

The first rays of the morning sun barely made it through the tiny window of Anuța's room. Although the room she had accepted the night before was small and dark, at least it was a permanent shelter for her and her little girl, and the strange woman that offered it seemed benevolent. With these thoughts Anuța got up from the simple bed and opened the small window that had not been washed for decades. A cool, fresh air filled everything. She did not manage to enjoy the refreshing air as the room's door banged against the wall and the old lady came through the threshold.

-*What are you doing, lass?* She hissed through her teeth. *Can't you see that you are spoiling the air in the house? That window is only for the light to come in, not for the air. Shut it at once!*

She shut the window immediately, but she was stunned for a moment. She wondered how the fresh and clean air could „spoil the air" in a house. The woman continued:

-*Come now we have work to do. You don't think you can stay here without doing anything!*

Anuța did not answer but took little Florentina by her hand and hurried out of the room.

-We will go in the forest at the foot of the Red Hill, after healing herbs and mushrooms. I will teach you the plants and their healing powers and if you learn obediently, one day everything that is here will belong to you, so stop being sad and let's get to work.

The sun was high on the horizon when the three of them started on the path that led to the forest. Anuța did not say anything but while on their way she asked:

-Auntie, you promised to bring my predestined one to me, the Prince from my dream. When did you think of doing this? I would be much quieter and more eager for life if I saw him.

The old woman did not answer but walking further she immersed herself in the thickets of the forest. The sun barely came through the rich foliage and only thin rays like spears touched the earth, which was covered with dry leaves. Here and there wildflowers and all kinds of weeds grew at random in small clearings, where the forest crown was not thick enough to stop the light. In shady places, dozens of mushrooms grew at the foot of ancient trees, taking their multi-coloured hats out of the bed of dried leaves. After a while they stopped, and the old wise woman began her lesson...

The day passed without notice and the sun was going to set when they started back towards the house. On the way the old woman blurted out:

-*Listen Anuţa, I like how you behaved today so tonight I will bring to you your predestined one as promised.*

-*Thank you kindly, auntie,* she said merrily.

She had no idea how this would happen, but she knew that **she loved** the Prince of her heart for a lifetime and that she would be his forever.

They got home and started at once, Anuţa made the fire and the old woman prepared the herbs and other things necessary for the spells. By using an ancient formula, she put everything on the fire and when everything that was needed was prepared, the old woman said:

-*Are you ready my dear to meet your **beloved** for the first time as you never have, not only to see him in your dream but even to touch him and **love him** as you always wanted?*

Anuţa did not reply. She was so impatient that her voice was completely gone. The old wise women lit a few green candles that suddenly filled the room with a yellow iridescent green light. This light dashed out of the windows, shedding a green ethereal light over the small garden. After that, she took a few hot coals from the hearth and put them on a tray at Anuţa's feet who was sitting straight and benumbed like a statue. The little Florentina fell asleep easily on a narrow bench in the darkest corner of the room. The old lady continued the ritual and taking a spoonful out of the broth she gave it to Anuṭa to drink. Then uttering an incomprehensible spell, she sprinkled the embers with the black liquid, using a small ladle to draw from the same concoction:

-ISCODEL, PRICONICEL

-PORANTOL, IMANCOL

-KOF, PUF, PAC, PIK

Shortly, out of the mist rising from the hot coals, first a black shadow started to take shape in the green light, and then in the thicker mist a silhouette could be distinguished which as time went on, became clearer and clearer.

Anuṭa was ecstatic with emotion and the concoction created in her an excitement without bounds. When the mist started to scatter in front of her, separated only by the tray with now completely extinguished coals, a young man appeared in scant attire that seemed to wear only a green robe down to his knees, a robe that clothed his athletic body. Anuṭa became breathless as she looked at him. It was the Prince from her maiden dreams.

In a warm and affectionate tone, he said:

*-Princess of my dreams, from my underworld kingdom I come in body to unite with you. **I love you** with all my heart and I will be yours for eternity.*

He held her tenderly by her waist and looking into her eyes kissed her passionately on the mouth. Anuța felt a knot in her throat and the words refused to come out of her mouth, but she answered the kisses as well as she could. He continued:

-I can be with you as many times as you want until the end of your life, but we can only meet and touch each other at night, because with the first ray of the sun my body will transform into ash, wherever I am.

Anuța came to her senses a bit and said:

*-Oh, **my beloved** Price, I cannot wish for more. If you are to be mine, every night, **I will love you** always till the end of my life.*

*-**My beloved**, that's how it will be but every time you wished for me to be with you, you must perform the ritual you saw tonight... and one more thing, after your death, your soul will be united with mine forever and in this way we will always be together. What do you say, will you agree to make a **covenant of love** with me?*

*-I will make the covenant with you if you promise me that you will **love me** in the same way even when I won't be as young and beautiful as I am today.*

*- I pledge **to love you** until the end of your days as much as today and then after death our souls will merge.*

-I pledge to be with you until death and after, as you said, finished Anuṭa.

He took her in his arms and led her to her room where they **made love** until morning. Anuṭa fell asleep happily for the first time in her life, and when she awoke the sun was already up in the sky. At the edge of her bed she found a small lump of ash like a cigarette ash.

The spell broke just as the Prince had said. They continued to live and love each other in this way for years on end. With time Anuṭa learned her trade from the wise women and came to do everything she knew. As for Florentina, she grew to be a rather tall and dry little lady, and because of her isolation and the modesty with which she behaved, she was not yet noticed by the village people.

There came the time when the old wise women fell ill. Anuṭa did everything she knew in order to prolong her life, but the laws of nature could not be broken. One evening the old lady called Anuṭa and Florentina to her bedside and told them:

-My daughters, I am going now. Now I can tell you my name that you never knew. My name is Maria, although the villagers call me Baba Rada. Just like you Anuṭa, I was also an apprentice to a wise woman whose real name I did not know, but the villagers also called her Baba Rada, and she also lived in this house. Anuṭa, the people in the village hardly know you at all, so when

I die, you should never say your name again, but call yourself like me, Baba Rada. If people are to ask you how you rejuvenated, you should say so: with herbs anyone can rejuvenate. Don't tell anyone that I'm dead, or it will be bad for you. As for you, Florentina, do the same when your mother Anuţa dies. Call yourself Baba Rada and let this name last forever. The dark forces will always be with you and will help you. Don't be afraid of anything and bury me under the walnut tree in the backyard...

This being said, Baba Rada took one last breath, snorted loudly, and then breathed her last. The two mourned their beneficent old wise woman, and they did exactly as she had asked.

At midnight they buried her in the backyard under the big walnut tree. When they dug, they found a pile of bones; a sign that all the wise women called generically „Baba Rada" were resting there...

Chapter 6

Dear reader, the Author is speaking to you now. What you will read in this chapter is a real story and, without knowing the two protagonists, I overheard their entire conversation when we once sat at tables next to each other in a completely empty restaurant. But let me tell you the events in the chronological order of their unfolding.

One Thursday I was out on a visit to my country Romania in a town called Timișoara (in the west of Romania). The reason was to visit a small spa town, in the neighbourhood called Buziaș, where I was going to attend my forty-year high school graduation reunion. Being hungry, I decided to go to have lunch at a restaurant in the centre of Timișoara.

Outside it was extremely hot and, although the terraces in the Opera Square looked inviting, I chose to dine in a cool underground place. The only restaurant with a cellar is of course the „Timișoreana" Restaurant, located in the former wine cellar from the communist era. I joyfully descended the steps, soaking in the pleasant coolness.

In the cellar main room, beautifully decorated with household objects and old photos, all representing the old Banat (region divided now between West Romania, North-East Serbia and South-East Hungary) households, I sat down at a table right in the middle. I wanted to have a treat and eat the famous Banat „sarmale" (meat rolls in pickled cabbage) with a spicy sausage and polenta. I had no idea what was to come. Being the only customer in the place at 11:45 in the morning, I was served in less than a minute with the wonderful „sarmale", but also with a cold and frothy pint of „Timișoreana" beer.

In the large plate sat six small „sarmale" next to a very fragrant spicy sausage, all placed on a bed of golden polenta. I sipped my cold beer and began to satisfy myself with my taste buds excited to the maximum.

While I was eating cabbage roll number three and was amazed at the speed with which everything disappeared in my rather wide belly, through the underground door of the restaurant appeared two picturesque characters, a **HE** and a **SHE**.

What followed was remarkable and judging by what you are about to read next, I think it's worth recording in a short story, obviously fictional, what I imagined happened before they entered the restaurant and what happened after they left. Obviously, the highlight is their discussion in the restaurant.

I was devouring the number three cabbage roll and watching them head resolutely towards my table. At one point I even wondered for a split second: do these people know me from somewhere, why come so determined towards me? I quickly repressed this fleeting thought and focused on giving them a better look. They were completely different in their style of clothing, but also in appearance and way of being. Let me briefly describe them:

HE, smaller in stature, brown and hairy, with a short haircut like a soldier from the communist era, with a narrow forehead and grey steel eyes buried deep in the head. Above his thin, barely contoured lips, sat a black moustache with the tips down, which looked clever. **HE** was in discoloured jeans, „rubbed with brick" as they said in my youth, and on his well-toned body **HE** wore a very tight white t-shirt so that his pectorals could be seen prominently and also the famous „six pack abs", the most coveted abs by both men, and even more so by some women. **HE** wore a thick chain around his neck and on his right hand a matching bracelet made out of solid gold. On his feet obviously white sneakers, all creating a general look of a contemporary douchebag.

    SHE, a tall, dry woman with a long but pleasant face. Her brown eyes with green iridescent flecks gave her an almost poetic look. Her lips were wide and slightly parted, as if enticing you to kiss her constantly. The small, barely contoured breasts gave her a virginal appearance, although the wide circles under her beautiful eyes were giving away the fact, **SHE** was no longer one. **SHE** had a flat, small, and „saggy" bum continued with invisible legs, impossible to assess, under a long skirt that crawled on the floor. As for clothing items, **SHE** wore a long-sleeved white knitted blouse made from synthetic acrylic, I suppose, on bare skin, and over this blouse, another kind of red „poncho" knitted from real wool. The skirt, as I said, was straight, black, and made of a synthetic material with a pattern embossed in the fabric. Its cut was like that worn by Baptist women when they go to their place of worship. This woman's gait was remarkably interesting, perhaps created by the illusion of the lack of legs; **SHE** seemed to glide on the white-black chessboard-like tiles of the restaurant floor. I cannot tell you what **SHE** had in her feet because I could not see them. **SHE** did not wear any jewellery on her hands or neck, and no earrings in her ears. Her light brown hair was cut short to her shoulders and it was combed backwards giving her a simple, sincere look. The lack of make-up and jewellery made her somehow unsophisticated, even simple, I might say.

As they walked next to each other, **SHE** always looked at him with admiration, unable to look away and **HE** only looked ahead, as if ignoring her completely. From the front, they looked like a couple joined randomly and not two people who had something in common. Walking resolutely towards my table, I wondered what would happen next.

I found out while having my fourth cabbage roll. They sat down right at the table next to mine, **HE** being next to me on my side less than two meters away and **SHE** in front of him and consequently in front of me.

There was a deep silence in the room, with no audio system or anything else that could have created an atmosphere. In that silence it was almost clear what the chatty cooks were talking about as they busied themselves with the food orders for the upstairs terrace. The chef's meat hammer and knife sang the „Restaurant Symphony for Hammer and Knife" in this deep silence. You must realize that in these exceptional acoustic conditions, everything my protagonists were going to discuss, I was going to hear.

The cabbage roll number four was almost finished when Clara, the small bodied waitress arrived eager to take their order. She gracefully placed in front of them the rather crumbling menus that they did not even bother to open. So far, no sound had been made except the squeaking and rustling of the chairs. **HE** said in a low voice:

-A beer...

SHE, a little bit more interested, said:

-A coffee!

Clara a little confused asked:

-What kind of beer?

The answer came promptly:

-A draught!

She no longer dared to ask, what kind of draught, what kind of beer, so sharp had been the reply of „our douche". After the atmosphere relaxed a little, in a few seconds, Clara asked again more confidently:

-And the coffee?

SHE replied:

-A single expresso, please.

Clara performed and impeccable „About Turn" as she „swept" the menus off the table with her right hand.

Ignoring what was happening at the next table, I continued to address the two tasty „sarmale" left on the plate. Their fragrant taste of thyme and dill, combined with the milky taste of polenta, made me forget for a moment the protagonists of my story. Absorbed by the wonderful taste sensations, I almost completely forgot what had happened. Especially since nothing special yet happened, only the picturesqueness of the characters and their behaviour struck me for a few minutes. I was really willing to forget everything and sipping the wonderful frothy beer I was transported to another world. Suddenly, **SHE** took me out of that sublime meditation. Before their beer and coffee came, **SHE** started talking slowly but loudly enough for me to hear everything.

-*Sweetheart,* **SHE** said, *you can't imagine how happy I am that you invited me to the restaurant. You know that until now no other man has invited me to a real restaurant. I was invited only to neighbourhood bars and miserable wineries in the country, but never to never to a restaurant in the centre of a big city like Timişoara and especially not to a restaurant with a tradition like this.*

Her rather strange, for me, opening ended abruptly and with a short and theatrical gesture **SHE** gripped his big tight fists in her little hands with long and delicate fingers. **SHE** leaned over the table, completely pressing her small breasts wrapped in the red poncho to the white tablecloth. Then **SHE** began kissing his fists with, for me, rather unimaginable passion! **HE**, annoyed, looked at me briefly and with a sudden gesture snatched his fists from her hands, leaving her parted lips longing for those big fists they wanted to kiss.

I admit that I was not polite at all - the scene amazed me so much that I stared like a fool, with the fork deeply inserted in the beginning of the sixth and last cabbage roll. When his gaze shot at me, I quickly turned my head to my tasty roll and with a studied and tactful gesture I began to swallow the remaining piece of the cabbage roll.

Out of the corner of my eye I was hoping to see her reaction. As quietly as **SHE** had begun, **SHE** continued her speech:

*-You know how much **I love you** my darling and I will always be grateful for what you did for me and especially for your wonderful gesture of inviting me here...*

Clara appeared speedily and **SHE** stopped her monologue. With a professional gesture she placed the coffee in front of her, hurriedly arranged the sugar and milk on a side plate and then put the Timișoreana beer mug in front of him, after which, feeling that she had interrupted something important, she slipped out of the landscape. **SHE** continued:

*-Forgive me **darling** for the early outburst but I am mad about you. I like to kiss you all over...*

Hearing that, I felt like I was drowning. I got a lump in my throat at the thought that in the empty restaurant I might be witnessing the „kissing everywhere" of a muscular body of a douchebag. I tried my best to get this fanciful thought out of my mind and, with difficulty, I managed to finish the last cabbage roll.

All I had left was the sausage attached to the „sarmale" and a little polenta to eat, while my brain, heated by the previous scene, began to fantasize like crazy. Some conclusions could already be drawn. The two protagonists were not from Timișoara, or at least one of them was not. But I could not locate where they were from, their bazaar clothing could place them anywhere, from Istanbul to Bucharest or even further from Timişoara. Another conclusion - their relationship was somehow just beginning, and **SHE** was extremely interested in its romantic side. As for him, I completely missed the nature of his interest in this relationship. With these thoughts in mind, I swallowed the delicious sausage as the protagonists of my story quietly sipped their beer and coffee.

Astonished by the silence that fell beside my table, I cautiously looked up from my plate, trying to take a look at the two of them.

SHE looked at him studying intensely over every feature of his face. **SHE** tried her best to catch his eyes, to capture his eyes with that miraculous „eye to eye" look when two souls merge into one with just one look.

HE much „earthlier", could not take his eyes off her virginal breasts. **HE** stared continuously, though her white knitted blouse was up to her neck and the red poncho covered everything. All that could be seen were two bumps, in truth, geometrically incredibly attractive.

After almost five minutes of silence, **SHE** put the cup down and was obviously unhappy that **SHE** couldn't catch his eyes in hers. **SHE** snapped:

-Why do you keep looking at my breasts?

HE shuddered and, quickly moving his gaze up to her face, apologized, whimpering almost like a child caught with his hand in the jar of candy:

-I wasn't looking at your breasts...

-Liar! **SHE** snapped. *Why are you lying to me* ***darling****? I know that you are attracted to my body...*

The conversation, as if taken from a cheap B type movie amazed me again. I could not believe that such a conversation could take place in a restaurant at noon where „sarmale" and sausages are eaten! Anyway, they were not eating, and maybe that coffee and beer suited the conversation, how should I know?

I allowed my gaze to slide back to the plate and the last piece of sausage and polenta disappeared into my greedy mouth, when the dialogue of absurd theatre, worthy of Eugen Ionescu (Romanian writer famous for Absurd Theatre), broke out again. **HE** said:

- Look what you did to me now... I have to go to the bathroom!

I could not believe what I was hearing. Sneakily I looked up again. With the sound of a chair being pulled aside, **HE** hurried to his feet and headed for the restroom located at the entrance of the restaurant. **SHE** looked at him as if satisfied, with an expression of someone who had just won the lottery „6 out of 49". After **HE** left the table

SHE got up in a hurry and with a professional gesture adjusted the handle of the bier mug, twisting it so that **HE** could easily grab it when he returned. Then **SHE** arranged his cell phone, tossed on the table, so that it was parallel to the edge of the table. Satisfied, **SHE** arranged her blouse and poncho a little bit to sit on her breasts as straight as possible. Then, taking out a small mirror and a tiny box, **SHE** dipped her little finger from her right hand into the box and slowly moved it over her fleshy lips, spreading a blush that gave her lips a moist, shiny appearance. **SHE** looked at me surreptitiously and, smiling, shook her head slightly from left to right, as if to say: „No, no, don't tell me... don't divulge my secret to **my lover**...” Then **SHE** sat down in her chair and sipped from her coffee, as if nothing had happened, while **HE** returned from the toilet visibly relaxed.

My plate being completely empty, I returned to the beer mug hoping that **HE** would not notice the amazement on my face that engulfed me as I was witnessing this absurd theatre. **HE** looked at her in her entirety and then sat down. **HE** grabbed the mug by the conveniently turned handle and took a deep breath. Then **HE** said:

*-Did you finish your coffee, **sweetie**?*

SHE chirped from her fleshy lips:

*-Yes **honey**!*

-Let's go then, **HE** said.

SHE stood up carefully and smoothed out a few invisible wrinkles from her non-crease black skirt and began to „glide like a queen" on the chessboard-like floor of the restaurant. **HE** walked one step ahead of her in the same way as **HE** did when **HE** came in, without looking back. I, in turn, was staring and trying to understand what all that meant... when suddenly, without expectation, **SHE** turned her head and looked me in the eye. Then, mimicking a barely outlined kiss, **SHE** smiled broadly. That topped it off. Now I really did not understand anything, and in addition to the lump in my throat, a strange heat was nestling at the base of my spine. Was it time for me to say the same as him: *Look what you have done to me now...? I must go to...*

I was struggling to get back into the real world when Clara shouted:

-Boss, boss, they left without paying, damn bastards!

Panting, she ran to the stairs and shouted:

-Ion, stop them, they didn't pay. It's the bumpkin woman in red with a black skirt; a coffee and a draught!

Tired, she approached my table and said in a low voice:

LOVE...?

- You have seen, Sir, how those wicked ones have gone. This week I have already paid 130 lei from my salary for bastards like these...

Dumbfounded, I asked for the bill and left her a huge tip. She thanked me and added that God is the only hope ... I agreed and came out into the light.

The heat in my back faded when my whole body was suddenly exposed to the stifling heat outside but, with had happened, my mind did not give me much peace. Where did these strange people come from and where did they go?

To find my peace, I had to write about them. I walked only a few hundred meters more and entered the Symphony Cafe near the Opera, where I took out my notebook and started writing while having a cold ice cream.

What came out you just read...

Anyway, I cooled down!

Chapter 7

After drinking up her coffee and his beer in a renowned restaurant in the big city, Florentina and Geo were now walking under the hot rays of the day star. She chirped:

*-Oh **honey**, how could we be so **in love** that we forgot to pay. Thank heavens they didn't call the Police and embarrass us, that would have ruined today's plans. What do you want to do now? You promised to take me to see the beautiful Rose Park. You know how much I like the roses. If you were a gentleman and I know that you are, I would like at least one rose, if not a whole bouquet.*

Geo did not reply, walking silently half a step ahead of her but at a leisurely pace without hurrying. She was silent, listening to the specific noise of the crowded centre. At last, in a hesitant voice, Geo said:

*-Florentina, **my sweetheart**, you know how much I want you; I can't wait to have you in the privacy of my home. If you would like to go to my place to eat something, take a shower, cool off before going to the park, then we could go to the park and along the river that flows alongside it. After that we will celebrate the wonderful day of today with a glass of champagne, and at*

dusk I will take you to the train station so that you can go back home to your village in the South-West.

His speech was interrupted by the unexpected flight of a flock of pigeons that almost struck them with their wings. Florentina laughed, but her body was aroused, thinking that she would not do anything wrong in respect to her lover, the Pastor, if she made love to Geo just once. Anyway, no one would know what happened between them because Geo was going to die soon. So, she unreservedly accepted his proposal, saying:

*- I know that my body attracts you a lot, but I'm crazy about you too. I want you desperately. Let's not tarry anymore and take a taxi, **honey**, what do you say?*

Geo smiled complicitly and said:

*-Oh, my dear Florentina, **I love you so**...*

They took the first taxi to his home. In the car, in the back seat, they began to kiss and explore each others bodies with feverish hands. Once there, they ate nothing. Clothes flew through the air, as did shoes. Naked, they ran into the large marble-clad bathroom. Cold drops of water fell on their hot bodies. A fine steam rose behind the glass screen, steaming it and making it impossible to describe **the images of love** for an outside observer. Judging by the short moans and screams mixed with the rain-like sound of the shower one could guess what was going on behind the screen. With a final roar, which seemed to be Geo's, the hot scene cooled, the sound of rain remained alone the entire sound background.

Happy, they ran naked to the large kitchen, where Geo hurriedly made up a cold snack using what he had in the refrigerator. Florentina, still under the aphrodisiac influence of the events that took place in the shower, was beginning to doubt **the love** she had for the Pastor. In fact, none of the men she had **loved** so far had made her feel like a woman, as had Geo. She watched him with real admiration, eagerly devouring the cold turkey steak with tomatoes and „Telemea" (Romanian traditional ewes' hard cheese). Gnawing at the last mouthful, Geo said:

*-**Honey**, excuse me a moment, I must make a phone call, I have a surprise for you.*

Geo retired to the master bedroom, sitting on the edge of the huge bed. He picked up his cell phone from the nightstand and ordered a bouquet of roses to be delivered in an hour to the well-known Rose Park. When returned to the kitchen he said:

*-All right **honey**, it's sorted. In an hour we must be in the Rose Park, as you wished, and there I have a surprise for you.*

*- Oh, **my sweetheart**, I also have a surprise for you, but I have to make a call too, if you don't mind...*

He laughed and said:

*-Florentina, **I love you**; how could I get upset? You can go to my bedroom and talk from there. It's the second door on the left...*

Florentina took her phone from her purse and, moving as lasciviously as possible, in only Eve's suit, disappeared into the huge bedroom. She called her **lover**, the Pastor, and told him to come to the Rose Park in less than an hour and wait hidden in the first boxwood bush at the entrance, which had a gap behind it. In that gap a man could hide without being seen. The Pastor laughed, saying:

*- **My love**, how diabolical you are, you couldn't find a more poisonous shrub to accomplish your mission...*

*-Yes, **honey**, I will lure him in such a way that he will turn his back on you when he will be pricked in the thorns of the roses that he will give to me. Then you will put out a hand behind his back and drip the potion made by my mother on his prickled bleeding fingers. And that's that, your dream come true...*

She came out of the bedroom a little baffled. Part of her wanted to stick to the bargain agreeing to be the Pastor's mistress the way she wanted, but another part **loved** Geo more and more. She quickly put aside these thoughts; otherwise the plan would have failed. She finally thought she would see on the spot what it would be like and decide then and there. She quickly entered the bathroom and arranged her face a little, after which she returned to the kitchen and chirped:

*-**Honey**, I am ready, the surprise is waiting for you also in the Rose Park.*

*- Oh! Let's go then, **sweetie**!*

They got dressed and ordered a taxi.

The afternoon sun shone brightly on the facades of historic buildings. Everything was enchanting. They reached the park and the taxi stopped. Geo paid gallantly and taking him by the arm Florentina felt that this was one of the happiest moments of her life. They entered the Rose Park and began to walk leisurely. The enticing scent of thousands of roses created an olfactory symphony, accompanied in harmony by a symphony of colours and shapes wonderfully chosen by the Great Creator. Florentina had never seen nor felt anything like it before. Geo said softly:

*- Florentina, your name evokes flowers in bloom and everything I feel now and here, among these wonderful flowers, I dedicate to you because **I love you**!*

Then in a corner of the park a boy appeared with a huge bouquet of roses in his hands. Geo gestured discreetly and said:

-***My love*** *let's go there* he said pointing to the boy; *the rose bouquet is for you!*

In the light of the setting sun, Florentina struggled inside, floating slowly at Geo's arm for the long-awaited surprise - the huge bouquet of roses...

Epilogue

*-My **sweetheart**, I'm hot, she said, bowing her head and blowing hard between her small breasts; let's go to that big boxwood bush at the entrance of the park and you can kneel in its shade. Then with a rose in your hand, the most beautiful in the bouquet, you can tell me how much you **love me**. What do you say?*

Geo performed this quickly. From the lovely bouquet he chose the most beautiful rose. Florentina headed for the bush at the entrance to the park. She knew that her **beloved** Pastor would be hidden in it. Her heart was pounding at the thought that in a few minutes Geo would be dead. The man who gave her the most wonderful sensations that a woman could feel, was going to die at her hands or more precisely because of her and the stupid commitment made in front of the young Pastor. She knew that he would be with his wife forever if the wife were to drink from the elixir prepared by her mother, so she could only be his mistress at most. Mixed thoughts ran through her head as she watched Geo pull out the most beautiful rose out of the bouquet and rest on one knee in front of the giant boxwood bush. She arrived smiling too. Geo in a determined voice began his declaration of **love**. Teeming with emotion and holding the rose, he said:

*- Florentina **my love**, you are the most beautiful gift that the Universe in its immeasurable greatness and abundance has given to me. **I love you so much** and I would **love you** to be my wife with all my heart. I wished...* and he stopped because one of the sharpest thorns of the rose went deep into his thumb.

He carefully removed the thorn, and a small droplet of red blood came out. The next moment a hand sprang from behind him and sprayed his finger with a blackish liquid.

Geo winced in astonishment, but he felt that his legs slowly stopped responding to him. He wanted to get up, but his body no longer obeyed him. Florentina watched the whole scene in astonishment. The Pastor was still hiding in the giant bush.

In less than a minute, with a last spasm, Geo crouched on the ground with the rose in his hand, then remained inert on the alley at the entrance to the park.

On that Thursday afternoon, there was no one in the park at that time; it was still early for couples or tourists who normally frequented the park.

Florentina, frightened by the whole affair, ran away desperately without touching him. She took the first taxi and went to the train station where she embarked the first train for her native village.

The Pastor soon left his hiding place and ran to take the same train, not knowing that Florentina was in it.

When the train reached the village in the South-West, they both saw each other in the almost empty station. The Pastor approached with small steps and said:

-*Thank you Florentina* and handed her the envelope with five hundred Euros.

-*I hate you*, she said taking the envelope.

He was somewhat dumbfounded, not understanding what had just happened.

- *I never want to see you again, and I won't come to your stupid church again! You can forget me. I don't think I will embrace any faith from now on... that was enough for me. I don't want to deal with men anymore!*

He interrupted her with a gesture, placing his index finger on her fleshy lips. The stationmaster was just entering the waiting room. He saw him and said:

- *Can I help you with something, brother Pastor?*

-*No, thank you,* said the Pastor, *I was just leaving. I came here to meet with Sister Florentina, she just returned from the city with some documents from our Union.*

-*I understand,* he said and came slowly out of the room.

Without saying another word, each went in his own direction. Florentina arrived home, tired, where her mother was hard at work mixing in the cauldron set on fire with healing herbs. Seeing her enter, she asked:

-Did you sort out what you'd promised to the Pastor?

Florentina did not answer but big tears began flowing from her large green eyes.

-My girl, if you want to be like me, you have to decide. You know that in the life of a wise woman there can be no men, no marriage, no children. I allowed you to get to know both the life of an ordinary woman and also the life of a wise woman. It looks like the time has come to choose...

With these words Anuța, now Baba Rada, ended her speech and returned to her boiling concoction.

Florentina stopped crying and staring at her mother she asked:

-Could you help me, mother?

-What do you want, my girl?

- I will serve you and, if you want to teach me everything you know, I will become the next Baba Rada. I think you understand now what I just chose.

A strange silence settled in for a few moments. Baba Rada did not answer and Florentina looked at her with dim eyes. Everything was now up to the old wise woman. At last she answered in a serious voice:

- My daughter, I experienced difficulties when I was like you, and now it's your turn. I need you to know that you fell pregnant today with that man, whom we both killed through the Pastor's hand. In nine months, you will give birth to a baby girl who may or may not be like us; just like you she will have to choose. As for her father, now dead, would you like to have him in the hollow nights just as I have my Prince? My master, the one who helps me in everything and with whom I will merge after death can help you too if you agree to give him your soul. What do you say?

*-Yes mother what can I say? Yes, Yes, Yes. **I love you** my dear mother....*

Florentina threw herself into her mother's arms where she remained in a long embrace.

The evening had long since set over the village in the South-West and the stars were already flickering enchantingly. Silence covered the whole village. From time to time a solitary bark recreated the impression of a deserted place. The lights on the windows of all the houses were off, just at the end of the village in the cottage at the foot of the Red Hill, a yellow iridescent green light combined with red light, flashed through the square windows.

LOVE...?

Life in the small village in the South-West followed its natural course coloured with „important news": „A famous „manelist" died of a heart attack, probably due to the heat, in a well-known park in the capital city".

But **love stories** always remained a constant, **people loving incessantly** each in his own way. **How many people, so many definitions of love...?**

As there are no **Love courses** in school, the perennial question remains... **LOVE...?**

-The End-